Girls Got Game

girls' **SOCCER**

Going for the Goal

by Lori Coleman

Consultant
Tracy Ducar
Founder and Director, Dynasty Goalkeeping
Former U.S Women's National Team Member

Capstone
press

Mankato, Minnesota

Snap Books are published by Capstone Press,
151 Good Counsel Drive, P.O. Box 669, Mankato, Minnesota 56002.
www.capstonepress.com

Library of Congress Cataloging-in-Publication Data
Coleman, Lori
    Girls' soccer : going for the goal / by Lori Coleman.
    p. cm.—(Snap books. Girls got game)
    Summary: "Describes soccer, the skills needed for it, and ways
to compete"—Provided by publisher.
    Includes bibliographical references and index.
    ISBN-13: 978-0-7368-6823-5 (hardcover)
    ISBN-10: 0-7368-6823-2 (hardcover)
    1. Soccer for women—Juvenile literature. 2. Soccer for children—
Juvenile literature. I. Title. II. Series
GV944.5.C65 2007
796.334082—dc22   2006023251

Editor: Kendra Christensen
Designer: Bobbi J. Wyss
Illustrator: Kyle Grenz
Photo Researcher: Charlene Deyle

Photo Credits: Capstone Press/Karon Dubke, 5, 8, 9, 10, 14, 17, 18, 19, 21, 23; Comstock Klips, back cover; Corbis/Duomo, 28; Corbis/Ed Bock, 7; Corbis/NewSport/Chris Trotman, cover; Corbis/Reuters/Eric Gaillard, 25; Corbis/Star Ledger/Tony Kurdzuk, 13; Getty Images Inc./Allsport Concepts/Nathan Bilow, 15; Getty Images Inc./The Image Bank/Larry Dale Gordon, 20; Getty Images Inc./Jonathan Ferrey, 27; Getty Images Inc./Stephen Dunn, 26, 29; PhotoEdit Inc./David Young-Wolff, 22

1 2 3 4 5 6 12 11 10 09 08 07

TABLE OF CONTENTS

CHAPTER ONE

GET OUT ON THE FIELD

In recent years, female soccer superstars like Mia Hamm have shown the world that girls can play soccer as well as, or better than, the boys. Just like you, these athletes first started playing soccer with friends at the park and on summer club teams. Girls all over the world can't help but get a thrill from watching a ball sail into the net.

Many great things can come from playing soccer. You can make new friends, get faster and stronger, and develop your soccer skills all at the same time. So grab your cleats, shin guards, and a ball, and get out on the field—you don't want to miss a minute of the excitement!

CHAPTER TWO

PLAYING BY THE RULES

With non-stop intensity crammed into 90 minutes, who wouldn't want in on the action? Soccer is a blast to play because the ball moves around so quickly. Both teams' players are constantly running, passing, and shooting. If the ball is flying toward her, a player may jump up and meet the ball with her head. Or maybe she'll trap the ball with her foot.

All this action isn't for nothing. Each team is trying to get the ball past the other team's goalkeeper and into the net. Soccer is usually a low scoring game, so each hard-earned goal is something to celebrate.

"A champion is someone who does not settle for that day's practice, that day's competition, that day's performance. They are always striving to be better.
—Briana Scurry, U.S. National Team goalkeeper"

Stick to the Basics

As with all games, soccer has a few rules to remember. The action starts with a kickoff in the center circle. Then, the players can move the ball with their feet, thighs, knees, or even heads. But only the goalkeeper can grab the ball with her hands. Even then, the keeper can only use her hands within the penalty area.

With both teams rushing for the ball, things can get physical. A player may be tempted to grab an opponent's jersey or give her a push. If this happens, the referee will call a foul and the other team will get a free kick. If a foul happens inside the penalty box, a player will face off with the keeper and shoot from the penalty mark.

Corner Kick

If a team is defending its' goal, and they cause the ball to go out over the end line, the opposing team will be awarded a corner kick. A corner kick is taken from the corner arc.

Goal Kick

If a player tries to shoot on goal, and the ball goes out over the end line, the defending team will get a goal kick. A goal kick is taken from the front edge of the 6 yard box.

Throw-In

A team gets a throw-in when the other team causes the ball to go out of bounds over the sideline.

Get into Position

To be the best player that you can be, you should learn more than one position. The more positions you experience, the better you will understand soccer.

Are you great at passing the ball right to the foot of your teammate? If so, you might have the aim it takes for the forward position. **Forwards** try to get in an area to take a shot on the goal.

Do you love running long distances? Then you might have the endurance that it will take to be a midfielder. **Midfielders** run up and down the field to help out on defense. They also help score goals.

Defenders, or fullbacks, try to keep the ball away from the goal area. They pass the ball to teammates up the field. Girls with powerful kicks make great defenders.

A soccer team's last line of defense is its **goalkeeper**. The keeper's job sounds simple—to keep the ball out of the goal. But the keeper has to react quickly when the ball comes at her.

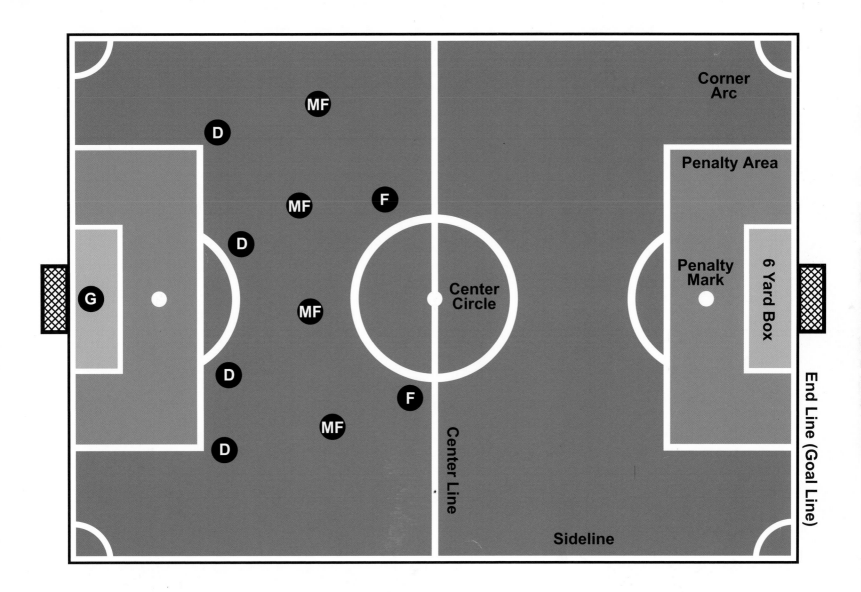

Corner Arc

Penalty Area

Penalty Mark

6 Yard Box

Center Circle

Center Line

End Line (Goal Line)

Sideline

G Goalkeeper **D** Defender **MF** Midfielder **F** Forward

CHAPTER THREE

SOCCER IN ACTION

Do you think soccer is the sport for you? Then it's time to pick a team. Most communities offer recreational soccer leagues. It's fun, low key, and you'll learn a ton about the sport.

Ready for the next level? In traveling programs, you will play teams from other communities. Teams that stand out may become premier or elite teams. These teams may travel around the region, or even around the country, to play other high-level teams.

Many teams host or travel to weekend or weeklong soccer tournaments. These tournaments are a fun way to pack a lot of soccer into a few days. Teams that keep winning play in championship games at the end of the tournament. They may go home with trophies or medals to honor their tournament success. No matter what the end result, playing with your teammates in a soccer tournament could be the highlight of your summer vacation.

Challenge Yourself

The more soccer you play and the more instruction you get, the better you will become. Attend soccer camps held in your community. These camps can last for one day or a whole week.

Here, coaches will help you zone in on what to practice. You may learn which position works best for you or learn a new drill. Knowing what you need to work on will prepare you for the next challenge.

Why not attend tryouts for a higher-level team? During a tryout, you'll be able to show your soccer talents. The coach might ask you to shoot on goal to see if you're the right fit as forward. You might be asked to play a practice game, called a scrimmage, to see how the team works together.

Even if you don't make the team the first time, you'll know what it takes to play at that level. Ask your coaches and instructors for feedback. Use their comments to set new goals for yourself as you improve your soccer skills.

Tryout Tips
- Get plenty of sleep the night before.
- Eat a good breakfast in the morning.
- Don't forget to drink lots of water.

15

Getting Schooled

Many school districts have teams for middle school and high school players. Some even have programs for younger players. While playing on a school team, soccer won't be your only challenge. Balancing soccer and your schoolwork takes just as much practice as getting the ball in the net. Being on a school team is a fun way to make friends, play more soccer, and show school spirit.

If you excel at soccer and school, you might want to check out the next step. Think about playing for a college team someday. Playing soccer in college has its perks. It's a great way to meet new people and make lasting friends. You could even receive a scholarship to play on the soccer team while attending classes. Who knows where soccer may take you in the future?

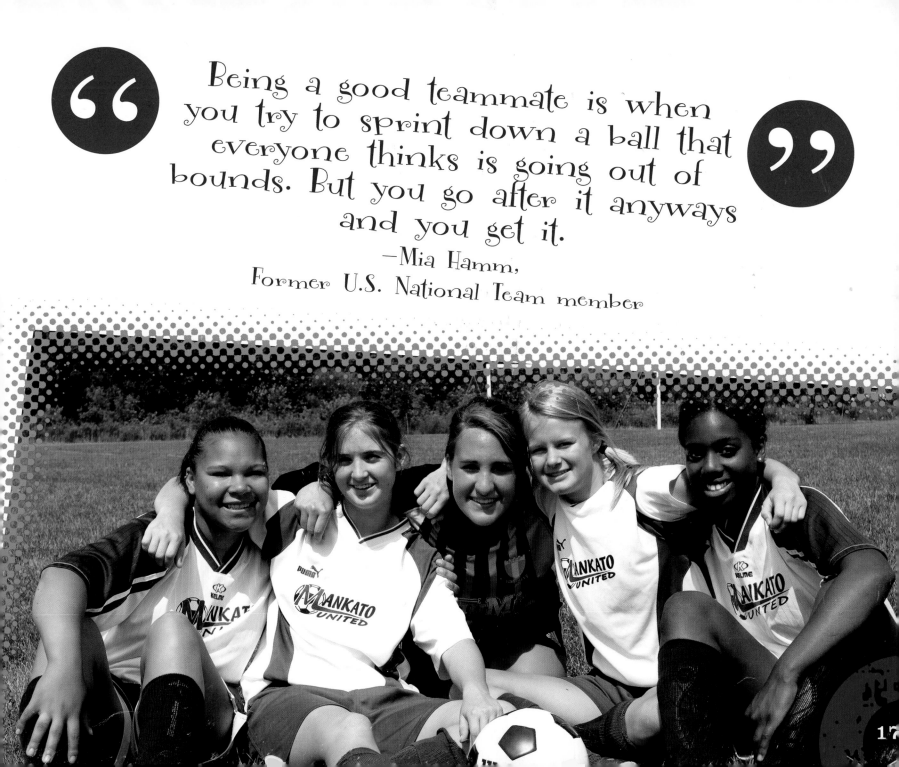

Being a good teammate is when you try to sprint down a ball that everyone thinks is going out of bounds. But you go after it anyways and you get it.

—Mia Hamm,
Former U.S. National Team member

CHAPTER FOUR

BECOMING THE BEST

Becoming a great soccer player takes more than running fast and having a powerful kick. To be the best, you need to stay on top of your game both on and off the field.

On the Field

When playing the fast-paced game of soccer, always be ready for that next explosive play. You want to be in the best position to attack the ball. Watch where your teammates and opponents are on the field. When the other team has the ball, make sure your opponents near you are covered. Then you can make a great defensive play.

When you have the ball, look up so you can see where players are moving. Practice this by dribbling around the field without looking at the ball. When you accomplish this, you'll be the player to beat!

Hydration Station

When working out, it's important to drink plenty of water. Water will refuel your body to last through a long soccer session.

- Drink lots of water before, during, and after exercise.

- Sports drinks and fruit juices can supply your body with extra carbohydrates and electrolytes, but most of the time they aren't necessary.

- Steer clear of drinks with caffeine, which dehydrates your body.

Off the Field

To improve your soccer skills, you'll want to spend time working out off the field. Activities that build endurance help you stay pumped throughout a 90-minute soccer game. Jogging, biking, and swimming are great ways to train your body to last through a long game.

You'll also want to improve your speed. Running up and down stairs or a hill builds strength in your legs. Sit-ups, crunches, and reverse sit-ups will strengthen your abdominal muscles.

Food for Fuel

When you're training for soccer, you want to feed your body the right things. Stay away from junk food. Before a practice or a game, choose foods that have a combination of carbohydrates and proteins. Carbohydrates provide your body with "right now" energy. Protein gives your body the long-term fuel to go the distance. Eat a meal about two hours before a serious workout.

Good Pregame Foods Include:

- pasta with tomato sauce
- yogurt with fruit and nuts
- fish and rice with veggies
- tuna and pasta salad
- peanut butter on crackers with veggies

Be a Good Sport

Soccer is an aggressive sport and it's easy to lose your cool when things don't go your way on the field. Sometimes people get mad at an opponent's push, frustrated with a referee's call, or upset about a coach's decision. You want to play your heart out, but don't let negative feelings get the best of you. At the end of the game, always line up to shake hands with the other team. Maybe ask the coach or referee a question if you don't understand something he or she did or said. But it's important to be polite and to accept the answer without complaining.

There's No "I" in Team

Let's face it. Soccer isn't just about getting the ball in the net. It's also about teamwork and communication. Help out your teammates on and off the field. During a game, try to get into a good position so they can pass to you. When you're at practice or after the game is over, help out by carrying the balls. Try being someone's partner for a drill. Soon you could have a teammate and a friend.

Hey, Big Shot!

Do you think that playing in the Olympics is a far-away dream? It might be closer than you think. There are camps all over the country that gear up players as young as 14 to show off their soccer skills. These camps are part of the U.S. Youth Soccer Olympic Development Program. At these camps, you can try out to make it on the national team for your age group.

If you make it to one of these teams, you could be playing in regional games against girls from all over the country. Your skills could even take you around the world playing against girls your age from other countries. But don't expect instant fame. It's a long process of tryouts and advice from coaches before you get that Olympic gold.

 Tomboy. All right, call me a tomboy. Tomboys get gold medals, tomboys can fly, and oh yeah, tomboys aren't boys.
—Julie Foudy,
Former U.S. National Team member

CHAPTER FIVE

PRO PLAYERS

The U.S. Women's National Team has rocked the world of soccer. They couldn't have done it without the skills and leadership of these amazing female athletes.

After joining the U.S. Women's National Team in 2001, Abby Wambach soon became a powerful force. In the quarterfinals of the Women's World Cup in 2003, she scored the game-winning goal to lead the U.S. to victory against rival Norway. Wambach was also part of the 2004 Olympic gold medal team. In 2006, she scored her 50th goal in only 64 games, making her the second quickest player in U.S. history to reach that mark.

Abby Wambach

Kristine Lilly

Kristine Lilly has played in more soccer games for her country than anyone else in the world—male or female. In January of 2006, Lilly played in her 300th game. As a midfielder, she has almost as many assists as she has goals scored. Lilly has played in three Olympic games, winning gold in two of them. She also is a two-time Women's World Cup champion.

Mia Hamm

Mia Hamm is probably one of the most famous athletes the United States has ever known, and for good reason. She is considered the best female soccer player in the world. Hamm started playing sports with her brother at a young age. She finally settled on soccer. When Hamm was only 15 years old, she became the youngest member of the U.S. Women's National Team. This team won the Women's World Cup when Hamm was 19. From that time on, she was a regular starter for the team. In December 2004, Hamm retired from the National Team. But she went out on top, scoring more goals than any other player in the world.

Briana Scurry has played more games for the U.S. Women's National Team than any other goalkeeper. Her save in a shootout in the 1999 Women's World Cup made way for the team to win the tournament. After six years as the national team's main goalkeeper, Scurry took a couple of years off. But she came back in 2002. She again started as keeper in the 2004 Olympic Games in Athens, where the U.S. team won the gold medal.

Briana Scurry

All of these famous soccer players would give you one piece of advice: if you want to get better at soccer, get out there and play! With some hard work and dedication, it won't be long before you are scoring goals or making saves yourself.

GLOSSARY

abdominal muscles (ab-DOM-uhn-ul MUHS-uhls)—the muscles on your belly; the stronger your core, or center of gravity, the more balanced and powerful you are.

carbohydrates (kar-boh-HYE-drates)—substances found in foods such as bread, rice, cereal, and potatoes that gives you energy

dehydrate (dee-HYE-drate)—not having enough water in your body

endurance (en-DUR-enss)—the ability of the body to work hard for long periods of time; regular physical exercise trains the body to increase its endurance, or stamina.

scholarship (SKOL-ur-ship)—a grant or prize that pays for a student to go to college or to follow a course of study

FAST FACTS

- U.S. Youth Soccer was founded in 1974. Since then, it has grown to be the biggest youth sports organization in the United States. More than 3.2 million kids play on teams that are part of U.S. Youth Soccer.

- The FIFA World Cup is soccer's biggest event. National teams from many different countries come together to play in this tournament. Billions of people around the world watch the games on television.

- Outside the United States, soccer is known as "football." But the term soccer really began in England. It came from abbreviating the term "association football," which became "assoc," then "socca," "socker," and finally "soccer."

READ MORE

Gifford, Clive. *Soccer Skills.* Boston: Kingfisher, 2005.

Wingate, Brian. *Soccer: Rules, Tips, Strategy, and Safety.* Sports from Coast to Coast. New York: Rosen, 2007.

Zarzycki, Daryl Davis. *Mia Hamm, Soccer Star.* Robbie Reader. Hockessin, Del.: Mitchell Lane Publishers, 2005.

INTERNET SITES

FactHound offers a safe, fun way to find Internet sites related to this book. All of the sites on FactHound have been researched by our staff.

Here's how:

1. Visit *www.facthound.com*

2. Choose your grade level.

3. Type in this book ID **0736868232** for age-appropriate sites. You may also browse subjects by clicking on letters, or by clicking on pictures and words.

4. Click on the **Fetch It** button.

Facthound will fetch the best sites for you!

ABOUT THE AUTHOR

Lori Coleman has been coaching community and high school soccer for more than ten years. During college, she studied in Spain, where she saw firsthand how hugely popular soccer is in other countries. Besides coaching, Lori likes to help kids out in school and in other sports like basketball, cycling, running, and horseback riding.

INDEX